Kaito's Cloth

Glenda Millard • Gaye Chapman

PHILOMEL BOOKS

Philomel Books

A division of Penguin Young Readers Group. Published by The Penguin Group.
Penguin Group (USA) Inc., 375 Hudson Street, New York, NY 10014, U.S.A. Penguin Group
(Canada), 90 Eglinton Avenue East, Suite 700, Toronto, Ontario M4P 2Y3, Canada (a division of
Pearson Penguin Canada Inc.). Penguin Books Ltd, 80 Strand, London WC2R 0RL, England. Penguin
Ireland, 25 St. Stephen's Green, Dublin 2, Ireland (a division of Penguin Books Ltd). Penguin Group
(Australia), 250 Camberwell Road, Camberwell, Victoria 3124, Australia (a division of Pearson
Australia Group Pty Ltd). Penguin Books India Pvt Ltd, 11 Community Centre, Panchsheel Park,
New Delhi - 110 017, India. Penguin Group (NZ), 67 Apollo Drive, Rosedale, North Shore 0745,
Auckland, New Zealand (a division of Pearson New Zealand Ltd). Penguin Books (South Africa)
(Pty) Ltd, 24 Sturdee Avenue, Rosebank, Johannesburg 2196, South Africa. Penguin Books Ltd,
Registered Offices: 80 Strand, London WC2R 0RL, England.

Library of Congress Cataloging-in-Publication Data available upon request.
ISBN 978-0-399-24797-2
10 9 8 7 6 5 4 3 2 1
First American Edition

For Shannon.

Even in winter the heart can fly. —GM

To Dick Weight, the love of my life;
and to Ando Hiroshige;
the landscape artists of China and Japan;
the Russian "Winter Palace";
and to "Willow Pattern" china. —GC

The Lord of Flight stood alone
on the Mountain of Dreams.

By moonlight he had worked making butterflies.
Now he waited for night's end
when he would float them,
one by one, upon the morning.

Kaito climbed the Way of Many Footsteps,
which led from her valley to the mountain.
From the crook of her arm swung a woven reed basket.

When at last she came to the end of the way,
Kaito bowed to the Lord of Flight
and asked his permission to step onto the mountain.

"What brings you here?" he asked.

"I have walked three days and nights, my Lord,
in hopes of watching my butterflies float
upon the morning one last time."

Kaito opened her basket, but when she saw
the shabby, faded butterflies, she began to weep.
"I am too late," she cried. "They have all died."

"Ah, Kaito, weep no more," said the Lord of Flight,
"for though their days were fleeting, your butterflies
have danced upon the breath of heaven and
have gladdened the hearts of all who saw them.
They have fulfilled the purpose for which I made them."

"What *is* the purpose of the butterfly?" Kaito asked,
and the Lord of Flight answered,
"Simply to fly. For it is flight that makes even
the plainest of them seem beautiful."

"Then why must they die so soon?"

"Only the wings are stilled. Flight is eternal.
It belongs to no one and to everyone.
We must learn to look for it in other places.
Come, sit with me and you will see it
in my new butterflies."

Kaito dried her eyes.

She sat with the Lord of Flight

upon the Mountain of Dreams

while morning came down all around them.

Then it was time for the floating to begin.

One by one, the Lord of Flight took the new butterflies

on his finger and raised them to the sun.

Gently he blew the gift of flight into their wings.

They trembled with the joy of it.
They floated and fluttered,
darted and danced and dived.

They gladdened the hearts of the valley people
who had woken early to catch a glimpse of them.
For winter drew near
and soon the butterflies would fly no more.

When the last of the new butterflies had flown,

Kaito asked,

"My Lord, could you make

my butterflies fly . . . just once more?"

The Lord of Flight shook his head.

"Not even I have the power to do that," he answered.

Kaito took up her basket.
Spring was far away and already she longed to see
the sky filled with the beauty of flight.

She bowed farewell to the Lord of Flight
and turned away from the Mountain of Dreams.

The Way of Many Footsteps,
which led to Kaito's valley home,
was long—three days long.
And three days was just long enough
for Kaito to have an idea.

She took a silver needle, as fine as a hair.

She threaded it with spiders' silk,

as strong as love and as soft as eiderdown.

She took a piece of cloth

as beautiful as a butterfly wing

and sewed it with ten thousand tiny stitches.

When at last she had finished,
Kaito once again began the long journey
to the Mountain of Dreams.

On the third day of walking, Kaito arrived.
White and silence covered the mountain.

The Lord of Flight looked down from the heavens.
"What brings you back, Kaito?"

"Winter is long," she said, "and the sky is empty.
But I think I have found a way to see flight
before the return of spring."

On the Mountain of Dreams,
Kaito spread the cloth she had sewn.
She slid twigs of bamboo
into the fine seams.

Then she raised the cloth
into the empty sky.

The Lord of Flight laughed.
Kaito's kite floated and fluttered,
darted and danced and dived
and rose high above the mountains,
filled with the gift of flight.